JEAN DE BRUNHOFF

THE STORY

OF

BABAR

the little elephant

Methuen Children's Books

Also by Jean de Brunhoff

Babar the King
Babar's Travels
Babar at Home
Babar and Father Christmas
Babar's Friend Zephir

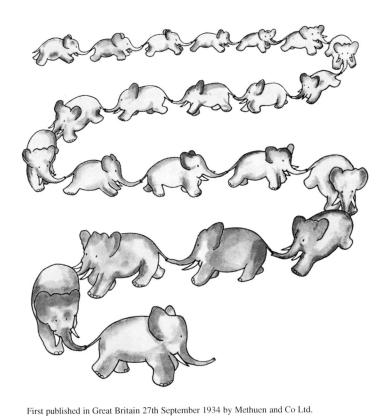

First published in Great Britain 27th September 1934 by Methuen and Co Ltd.
First published in Paperback format 1995 by Mammoth
Reissued 1999 by Methuen Children's Books
an imprint of Egmont Children's Books Limited
239 Kensington High Street, London W8 6SA
This edition first published in 2000 for The Book People Ltd, Hall Wood Avenue, Haydock, St Helens WA11 9UL
L'histoire de Babar
Copyright © Librairie Hachette, Paris
All rights reserved

3 5 7 9 10 8 6 4 2

ISBN 0 7497 3759 X

Printed in the U.A.E.

In the Great Forest
a little elephant was born.
His name was Babar.
His mother loved him dearly,
and used to rock him to sleep
with her trunk,
singing to him softly the while.

Babar grew fast. Soon he was playing
with the other baby elephants.

He was one of the nicest of them.
Look at him digging in the sand with a shell.

One day Babar was having a lovely ride
on his mother's back,
when a cruel hunter,
hiding behind a bush,
shot at them.

He killed Babar's mother.
The monkey hid himself, the birds flew away,
and Babar burst into tears.
The hunter ran up
to catch poor Babar.

Babar was very frightened
and ran away
from the hunter.
After some days,
tired and footsore,
he came to a town.

He was amazed,
  for it was
  the first time
he had ever seen
so many houses.

What strange things he saw!
Beautiful avenues!
Motorcars and motorbuses!
But what interested Babar
most of all was
two gentlemen
he met in the street.

He thought to himself:
"What lovely clothes they have got!
I wish I could
have some too!
But how can I get them?"

Luckily, he was seen by
a very rich old lady
who understood
little elephants,
and knew at once
that he was longing for
a smart suit.
She loved making others happy,
so she gave him her purse.

"Thank you, Madam,"
said Babar.

Without wasting a moment
Babar went into a big shop.
He got into the lift.
It was such fun
going up and down
in this jolly little box,
that he went ten times to the very top
and ten times down again to the bottom.

He was going up once more
when the lift-boy said to him:
"Sir, this is not a toy.
You must get out now
and buy what you want.
Look, here is the shop-walker."

Then he bought

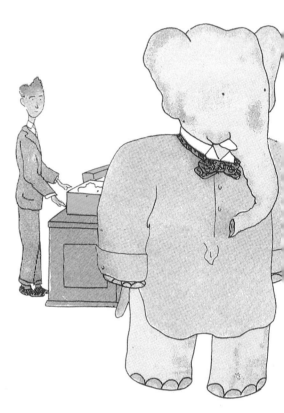

a shirt,
collar
and
tie,

a suit
of a
delightful
green
colour,

next
a lovely
bowler
hat,

and
finally
shoes
and
spats.

Babar was so pleased
with his purchases,
and satisfied
with his appearance
that he paid a visit
to the photographer.

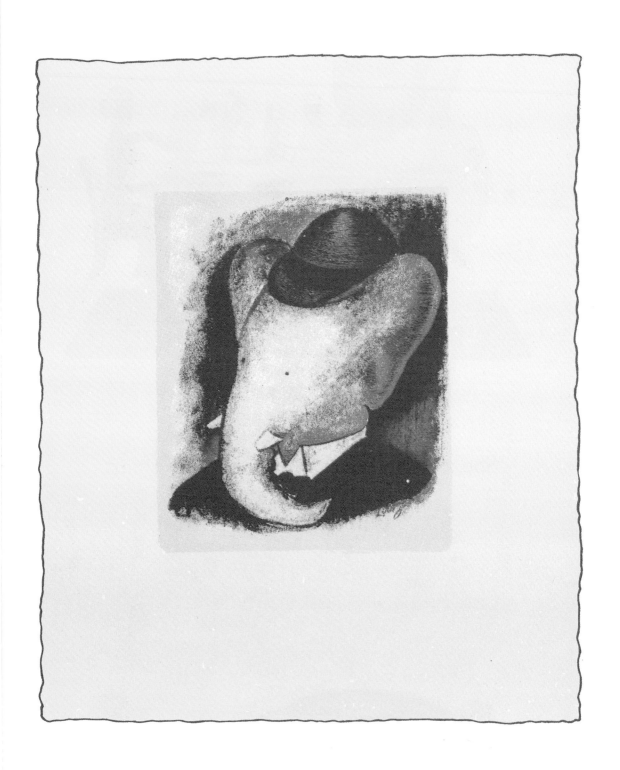

And here is his photograph.

Every day he drove out in the car
that the old lady had bought him.
She gave him everything that he wanted.

A learned professor gave him lessons.
Babar was attentive,
and always gave the right answer.
He was a most promising pupil.

In the evenings, after dinner,
he told the old lady's friends
all about his life in the Great Forest.

And yet
Babar was not altogether happy:
he could no longer play about
in the Great Forest
with his little cousins
and his friends the monkeys.
He often gazed
out of the window
dreaming of his childhood,
and when he thought of
his dear mother
he used to cry.

Two years passed by.
One day he was out for a walk,
when he met two little elephants
with no clothes on.
"Why, here are Arthur and Celeste,
my two little cousins!"
he cried in amazement to the old lady.

Babar hugged Arthur and Celeste
and took them to buy some lovely clothes.

Next, he took them to a tea-shop,
where they had some delicious cakes.

Meanwhile in the Great
Forest all the elephants
were searching for Arthur
and Celeste
and their mothers grew

more and more anxious.
Luckily, an old bird flying over
the town had spied them, and
hurried back to tell
the elephants.

The mothers went to the town
to fetch Arthur and Celeste.
They were very glad when they found them,
but they scolded them all the same
for having run away.

Babar made up his mind
to return to the Great Forest
with Arthur and Celeste and their mothers.
The old lady helped him to pack.

When everything was ready for the journey
Babar kissed his old friend good-bye.
If he had not been so sorry to leave her
he would have been delighted to go home.
He promised to come back to her,
and never to forget her.

Off they went!
There was no room
for the mother elephants
in the car.
So they ran behind,
lifting their trunks
so as not to breathe in the dust.
The old lady was left alone,
sadly thinking:
"When shall I see my little Babar again?"

Alas! That very day the King of the elephants
had eaten a bad mushroom.

It had poisoned him. He had been very ill,
and then had died.
It was a terrible misfortune.

After his funeral
the oldest elephants met together
to choose a new King.

Just at that moment they heard
a noise and turned round.
What a wonderful sight they saw!
It was Babar arriving in his car,
with all the elephants running and shouting:
"Here they are! Here they are!
They have come back!
Hello, Babar! Hello, Arthur!
Hello, Celeste!
What lovely clothes!
What a beautiful car!"

Then Cornelius,
the oldest elephant of all,
said, in his quavering voice:
"My dear friends, we must have a new King.
Why not choose Babar?
He has come back from the town,
where he has lived among men and learnt much.
Let us offer him the crown."

All the elephants thought
that Cornelius had spoken wisely,
and they listened eagerly
to hear what Babar would say.

"I thank you all," said Babar;
"but before accepting the crown I must
tell you that on our journey in the car
Celeste and I got engaged to be married.
If I become your King, she will be your Queen."

Long live Queen Celeste!
Long live King Babar!!

the elephants shouted with one voice.
And that was how Babar became King.

"Cornelius," said Babar,
"you have such good ideas
that I shall make you a general,
and when I get my crown
I will give you my hat.
In a week's time
I am going to marry Celeste.
We will give a grand party
to celebrate our marriage
and our coronation."
And Babar asked the birds
to take invitations to all the animals,

and he told the dromedary to go to the town
to buy him some fine wedding clothes.

The guests began to arrive.
The dromedary brought the clothes
just in time for the ceremony.

After the wedding and the coronation

everyone danced merrily.

The Party was over.
Night fell, and the stars came out.
The hearts of
King Babar and Queen Celeste
were filled with
happy dreams.

Then all the world slept.
The guests had gone home,
very pleased and very tired
after dancing so much.
For many a long day
they will remember that wonderful ball.

Then King Babar and Queen Celeste
set out on their honeymoon,
in a glorious yellow balloon,
to meet with new adventures.